WALT DISNEY'S

Bambi

MOUSE
WORKS

Squirrel stretched and yawned as the sun rose over the forest and its first rays lightly touched the top of the big tree where he lived. It was springtime. Leaves were sprouting everywhere. And someone was shouting at his neighbor, the owl.

"Wake up, Friend Owl," said the excited voice.

"Hey! What's going on here?" grumbled Owl, as he hopped onto a tree branch and looked down.

A young rabbit sitting on a fallen tree shouted up at him. "It's happened. The new prince is born! We're going to see him."

Owl blinked sleepily and then flew off after the rabbit.

Squirrel scampered down
the tree and told a field
mouse the good news. "The
new prince has been born,"
he said.

The mouse told the raccoon.
The raccoon told the moles. The
moles told the opossums, the
quail, and the wrens.

Soon every animal in the
forest was on its way to see
the new prince.

"Quick, quick," twittered
two flying birds.

"Hurry, hurry," repeated the
raccoon.

"He's been born. He's been
born," they all sang.

Everyone crowded around
the thicket trying to get a
glimpse of the little fawn
sleeping next to his mother.

"Isn't he precious?"
whispered the bluebird.

"Oh, my," squawked the
woodpecker.

"Shhhhh," hissed the
raccoon. "Don't wake him."

"You're to be congratu-
lated," boomed Owl.

"Congratulations,
congratulations," said all the
animals.

The doe lowered her eyes.
"Thank you very much,"
she said.

The fawn's mother gave him a tender caress. The fawn opened his eyes and looked around.

"Wake up! We have company," said his mother.

"Hello, little prince," said the animals.

The young rabbit hopped up to the new fawn and looked at him closely. "Whatcha gonna call 'im?" he asked the doe.

"I think I'll call him Bambi," she said.

"My name is Thumper," said the rabbit, and he thumped his hind leg to show her how he got his name.

For a moment Bambi looked a little frightened. Then he
tried to stand. At first his legs wobbled, but soon he could
stand straight and strong.

As Bambi got older, he and Thumper walked along the
leafy paths of the forest finding new surprises every day.
The forest was filled with friends. And they all stopped to
visit with the new prince.

Mother Quail brought out her new family to see the young fawn.

Mother Opossum saw Bambi coming down the forest path.

"Good morning, young prince," she said.

"Good morning, young prince," chorused her babies.

Bambi stopped and tried to look at them. He turned his head around so he could see them upside down. There certainly were many different kinds of animals in the forest.

Thumper showed Bambi all sorts of new things and told him their names.

"Those are birds," said Thumper.

"Bir-r-ds," Bambi repeated.

When a butterfly landed on Bambi's tail, he proudly called out, "Bird, bird."

"That's not a bird," giggled Thumper. "It's a butterfly."

The butterfly flew into a patch of flowers. "Butterfly,"
said Bambi, nosing the flower.

Thumper giggled again. "No, Bambi," he chuckled.
"That's a flower."

When Bambi bent down to sniff the flower, he found himself nose to nose with another animal.

"Flower," he called proudly.

Thumper burst out laughing. "No, Bambi. That's not a flower. It's a skunk."

"Aw, he can call me Flower if he wants to," said the little skunk shyly.

A sudden clap of thunder sent the little skunk back into the flowers. "We'd better get home," said Thumper as they both ran for cover.

Bambi nestled close to his mother under the thicket
while the gentle rain fell on the forest. Thumper snuggled
deep in his warm burrow. The squirrels in the trees
wrapped themselves in their big, furry tails.

And the little birds in the nest huddled under their mother's wing, which she spread over them like a big umbrella.

One day Bambi's mother
took him to the meadow.

"What's a meadow?" asked
Bambi.

"It's a wonderful place," said
his mother, "and I think you're
big enough to see it now."

Bambi followed her to the edge of the forest, where she made him wait.

"You must never rush out on the meadow," she told him. "There might be danger. The meadow is wide and open, and there are no trees or bushes to hide us. We have to be very careful."

When she was sure that it was safe, she stepped out onto the meadow. Then she called for Bambi and together they raced through the grass—just for fun.

Bambi's mother came to a stop and lowered her head to eat the sweet meadow grass.

Bambi nibbled a few blades, but it didn't taste good to him, so he left his mother to join the rabbit family, who were happily munching a mound of clover not far away.

"Eat the flowers," said Thumper. "The green stuff tastes awful."

Bambi pushed his nose deep into the clover and
suddenly something sprang out and landed on a rock.
Bambi followed it and put his nose down next to it again.

"Watch out!" it croaked, and it disappeared into the pond.

"That's a frog," said Thumper.

Bambi put his nose down next to the water to look for
the frog. As he bent over, he saw another fawn exactly like
himself. "What's that?" he asked.

"It's only you," giggled Thumper. "It's called a reflection."

As Bambi stared at his reflection, he saw another fawn looking back at him. Now there were two reflections in the pond.

"Hello," said the reflection. It was a baby doe. "My name is Faline. Would you like to play with me?" she asked. Turning suddenly, she ran through the meadow, hoping Bambi would follow.

Bambi began running, too, but in his excitement, he tripped and fell in the water.

Faline turned around to look for Bambi and saw him sitting in the pond. "C'mon, Bambi," she coaxed. "Play tag with me."

Soon Bambi and Faline were playing happily together, chasing each other around their mothers as if they had always been friends.

Suddenly they heard hoofbeats. A herd of stags came galloping across the meadow, led by the Great Prince of the Forest. The Great Prince turned and looked straight at Bambi.

Bambi drew closer to his mother. "He's looking at me," he said.

"Yes, I know," said his mother. "He's your father, and everyone respects him. Of all the deer, not one has lived half so long. He's very brave and wise. That's why he's known as the Great Prince of the Forest."

Bambi lowered his eyes, but he could still feel his father's gaze. He felt small compared to this majestic stag with his great antlers. He silently hoped that one day he would be as strong and wise as the Great Prince.

The silence was shattered by
the frightening noise of a
gunshot. The Great Prince
raised his head and shouted a
warning.

"Man is in the forest!" he
cried.

The herd of stags thundered
past Bambi.

Bambi shrieked, "Mother,
where are you?"

He could hear his mother
calling, "Bambi, Bambi!"

All the animals were running from the meadow and
Bambi ran with them. Soon he heard his mother's voice
behind him urging him on. "Bambi, hurry! Hurry!"
Another shot rang out. It seemed to be getting closer.
Bambi ran as fast as he could, but he was getting tired.
"Faster! Faster!" shouted his mother.

"Follow me, Son" said a voice. It was the Great Prince, and he led them to the safety of a dense thicket. Bambi and his mother stayed there until they could no longer hear the thundering noise of the gun. Soon the forest was quiet again.

When Bambi's mother was sure the hunters had gone,
they came out of the thicket. The Great Prince had
vanished.

"Where did he go?" asked Bambi as his mother led
him back to their home in the heart of the forest.

"I don't know," said his mother, "but I'm glad he
was there."

One morning Bambi woke up to find the world had turned white during the night. Every blade of grass was covered with a cold, white coat, and so was every tree and bush.

"It's snow," his mother said. "You can step on it."

Bambi heard Thumper calling from the frozen pond. "Come on, Bambi," he cried. "The water's stiff." Bambi raced through the snow down to the edge of the pond and stepped out on the ice. But his front legs shot forward and his back legs slipped from beneath him. Down he went with a thud.

Thumper slid up to him. "Maybe we should play somewhere else," he laughed.

Bambi and Thumper had a fine time playing in the snow. They raced up and down the icy hills until they tumbled into a snowbank. They could hear a faint snore from beneath the bank, where their friend Flower was asleep in his den.

"He's hibernating," explained Thumper. "Skunks always sleep right through the winter."

Winter was a lot of fun, but as time went on, there was less and less food. All the animals were hungry. The squirrel had stored food, but as winter wore on, even his supply grew short. Bambi and his mother would paw the ground looking for plants or grass under the snow. And when that was gone they would eat the bark from the trees.

One day Bambi's mother found a few blades of new grass. As Bambi nibbled hungrily, she lifted her head to listen. Then Bambi heard a shot. It was Man again.

"Run for the thicket, Bambi," his mother called. "And don't look back."

There was another shot from Man's gun. Bambi ran, heart pounding, until he reached the thicket.

He waited, but his mother never came. Instead, the Great Prince appeared beside him. "Your mother can't be with you anymore," he said. "Now you must be brave and learn to walk alone."

Bambi looked sadly back at the thicket once more, then followed the Great Prince into the forest.

At last the long winter was over. The snow melted and everything began to change. Flowers were blooming and the trees were tipped with leaves and buds. Flower the skunk awoke from his long winter sleep and came out of his den.

Thumper sat underneath a tree and thumped his foot. The birds twittered excitedly overhead as Bambi, now a handsome buck, sharpened his new antlers on the tree.

"Hey! Hey! Stop that racket!" called Owl. "Shoo! Scat! Can't a body get some sleep?" he shouted, trying to put his head under his wing. The tree continued to shake and Thumper thumped louder.

"Get out of here!" shouted Owl. Then he looked down in surprise. "Why, it's the young prince, Bambi. My, my, how you've changed," chuckled Owl. "Turned your spots in for antlers. It won't be long before you're twitterpated."

Bambi didn't understand what Friend Owl meant until one day when he was walking alone in the forest. Suddenly, he wasn't alone anymore. Standing next to him was a beautiful doe.

"Do you remember me, Bambi?" she asked. "I'm Faline." She gently licked the side of his face.

"This must be twitterpated," Bambi thought dizzily as he followed Faline down the forest path.

Bambi and Faline followed the path to the top of the hill.
The grass was blowing in the gently breeze. Bambi had never
been so happy. He jumped up on his hind legs and bounded
down the hill, leaping through the meadow and springing into
the pond. Then out of the pond and around the meadow he
ran, with Faline following close behind.

At last, tired and breathless, they stopped to rest next to
the trees near the waterfall. Bambi was in love. He closed
his eyes dreamily, but the sound of a deep voice made him
open them in surprise.

"Not so fast," said another young buck. It was Ronno. "Faline is coming with me," he said as he ran between them and began nudging Faline down the path. She looked back anxiously at Bambi.

"No, she's not," said Bambi as he lowered his head and butted Ronno with all his might.

Ronno turned and the two bucks ran toward each other, locking antlers and rearing up on their hind legs.

Again and again they crashed into each other, butting heads and tangling antlers.

Finally, Bambi raced at Ronno. Locking antlers, he used all his strength to throw the powerful young buck to the side.

Ronno squealed in terror as he fell and rolled down a bank into the river below.

Beaten at last, Ronno limped off into the forest. Bambi watched him go, then called for Faline to join him. Now there was nothing to keep them apart.

One morning Bambi sensed danger in the forest. He stopped and looked about cautiously. He climbed to the top of a hill and saw smoke rising from a campfire.

"It's Man," said a voice. Startled, Bambi looked up to see the Great Prince. They looked down together. "There are many of them this time," said his father. "We must go deep into the forest."

News spread quickly. All the animals ran to hide.
Thumper gathered his family together in the safety of their
burrow. Flower joined his family in their underground den.

Faline ran through the forest. "Bambi!" she called in terror. She could hear the sound of dogs barking behind her, and she could tell they were getting nearer.

Faline stopped calling for Bambi and ran for the safety of the cliffs, but before she could reach them, a pack of hounds burst out of the bushes behind her. Snarling and biting, they chased her as she made her way to the bare cliffs. Once there, she struggled up the steep slopes, the dogs still snapping at her heels.

Panting and out of breath, Faline was sliding backward when she heard a yelp. Bambi had burst out of the forest and was charging one of the biggest dogs. The pack scattered, snarling and barking, as Bambi held them off so Faline could scramble up to safety at the top of the cliff.

As Bambi fled from the dog pack, with Faline in front of him, the roar from a gun knocked him to the ground. His shoulder burned with pain and he lay still, too tired to move. He no longer cared what happened to him.

Suddenly, the Great Prince was by his side urging him to stand.

"You've got to get up," he said. "You've got to run. The forest has caught fire from Man's camp. We'll be safe in the river."

Bambi struggled to his feet and started to run.

The forest was ablaze. Trees were falling and heavy black smoke made it hard for Bambi to breathe, but his father kept him going. When they came to the river, they both jumped into the rushing water and swam with all their might to the edge of the falls. "We'll have to leap over," called his father.

They both disappeared over the edge of the falls, just as a huge burning tree crashed into the water behind them.

In a sheltered glade down the river, Bambi and the Great Prince dragged themselves from the water.

"Bambi!" called Faline, as she ran to greet him and gently licked his wounded shoulder. "I'm so glad you're safe."

That night Bambi and Faline watched together as the fire burned through their forest home.

In the morning light they could see that everything was black and bare—no leaves, no flowers, no grass. But Man was gone.

One by one the animals returned to the fire-blackened forest and began to rebuild their homes. Thumper scratched out a new burrow. Flower repaired his den. And the moles dug new tunnels in the scorched earth.

After winter, the forest came to life again. New leaves
and flowers grew, and grass covered everything once more.
Baby moles poked their heads out of the soft earth. A new
litter of baby skunks crawled out of the bank, and a new
family of rabbits raced around the meadow.

There was something else new in the forest that spring. The squirrel looked up from gathering acorns as Thumper raced by, followed by his new family.

"Wake up, wake up, Friend Owl!" shouted Thumper.

"Wake up! Wake up!" chorused his new babies.

"Oh, what now?" grumbled Owl, poking a sleepy head out from beneath his wing.

"It's happened! In the thicket!" yelled Thumper. "Come and see."

Owl flew after him.

The squirrel scampered down the tree and told a field mouse the good news. The mouse told the raccoon. The raccoon told the moles. The moles told the opossums, the quail, and the wrens. And soon every animal in the forest was on its way to the thicket.

As they drew close, the animals lowered their voices.

"Shhh, don't make so much noise," said Thumper.
Then he rubbed his eyes.

"Look," he said. "There are two of them."

Faline looked up from the thicket. Lying beside her were two fawns.

"Prince Bambi ought to be mighty proud," hooted Owl. "I don't believe I've ever seen a more likely-looking pair."

"Thank you," said Faline as she lowered her eyes and gently licked her two babies.

Bambi stood with his father on the hill overlooking the valley where Faline lay with the new fawns. The old stag turned quietly and disappeared into the forest, while Bambi stood regal and proud, the new Prince of the Forest.

The cycle of life in the forest had begun again. Thumper the rabbit and his family would grow sleek on rich, fragrant clover, and Flower the skunk and his little ones would feed in the bright fields of flowers. They would all watch Bambi and Faline teach their fawns the ways of the world, just as Bambi himself had learned them, so long ago.

Published by Penguin Books USA Inc., 375 Hudson Street, New York, New York 10014
©1993 The Walt Disney Company. All rights reserved. No part of this publication may be reproduced, stored in a
retrieval system, or transmitted in any form, by any means, electronic, mechanical, photocopying or otherwise,
without first obtaining written permission of the copyright owners.
Mouse Works is a registered trademark of The Walt Disney Company.
Printed in the United States of America.

ISBN 0-453-03080-7

10 9 8 7 6 5 4 3 2